James Edmund Harting

Hints on Shore Shooting

James Edmund Harting

Hints on Shore Shooting

ISBN/EAN: 9783743435582

Printed in Europe, USA, Canada, Australia, Japan

Cover: Foto ©Andreas Hilbeck / pixelio.de

More available books at **www.hansebooks.com**

SHORE BIRDS.

HINTS

ON

SHORE SHOOTING;

WITH A CHAPTER ON

SKINNING AND PRESERVING BIRDS.

BY

JAMES EDMUND HARTING, F.L.S., F.Z.S.,

AUTHOR OF "THE BIRDS OF MIDDLESEX," ETC. ETC.

LONDON:

JOHN VAN VOORST, PATERNOSTER ROW.

1871.

LONDON :

PRINTED BY WOODFALL AND KINDER,

MILFORD LANE, STRAND, W.C.

CONTENTS.

PREFACE.

SOME of the following chapters have already appeared in print in the shape of articles contributed to different periodicals. Others have never been previously published. They embody the result of the Author's personal experience in a pursuit to which, for many years, he has been devoted; and hence no statement is made the accuracy of which has not been repeatedly tested.

The descriptions and measurements of the birds have been taken from a very large series in the Author's private collection, and may therefore be relied upon as correct.

With the view of imparting instruction to some, and amusement to others (those who, like himself, have gone over the same ground with the same enthusiasm), the Author now commends these Notes to the perusal of sportsmen and naturalists.

HINTS

ON

SHORE SHOOTING.

CHAPTER I.

WHERE TO GO, AND WHAT TO TAKE WITH YOU.

THOSE who have been much upon our coasts know that there are two different kinds of shores; that which slopes down to the sea with a gentle declivity, and that which rises with a precipitate boldness, and seems set as a bulwark to repel the force of the invading waves.

The class of birds which haunts the one is very different to that which frequents the other. If you would observe the web-footed birds—the gulls, puffins, guillemots, razor-bills, and cormorants—you

B

should visit the rugged limestone rocks or white
chalk cliffs; if you would study the long-billed, long-
legged wading birds, you must seek the oozy mud-
flats or the glistening sands. It is the latter birds
which now engage our attention; with the former
the shore shooter has no concern.

Nothing can be more unsportsmanlike or more
inhuman than to shoot gulls and puffins by the
score from the rocks. To the majority of shooters
they are useless when killed, and no one deserving
of the name of sportsman should countenance the
wholesale destruction of birds whose confiding
nature and gregarious habits render them such easy
victims to the gun, and whose beauty and utility are
wrested with their life.

By " shore shooting, " then, is here intended
the pursuit of the various species of plovers and
sandpipers which frequent our shores and tidal harbours, and which, by reason of their exposed haunts,
extreme wariness, and rapid flight, test the crafty
powers of the fowler, his judgment and strength in
stalking, and his skill in shooting.

Many sportsmen who delight in a long day's
partridge-shooting, and who would walk miles to

join in a good " battue," speak with contempt of what they are pleased to term " shore popping."

The reason is pretty obvious; they have either never tried it, or have never been very successful in their attempts. The style of shooting is so different to that to which they have been accustomed, that they miss more frequently than hit; or, if they lack no skill in aiming, they are prevented from exercising it for want of a knowledge of the habits of the birds, and the requisite skill to approach them.

Again, the man who is wedded to a turkey-carpet and an elaborate *cuisine*, cannot stand the sanded floor and eggs-and-bacon at a remote seaside inn. He grumbles at the notion of having to clean his own gun and grease his own boots, and wonders what amusement can be found in shivering with cold in a punt, or wading knee-deep in mud, for the sake of a few golden plovers. All we can say is— " try it." After the monotony of a month's partridge-shooting, the change is delightful. As a receipt for health and strength there is nothing like it, and when you have once become acquainted with the haunts and habits of the birds, and

know how to get at them, the sport is most
fascinating.

Above all, the variety of species to be met with,
and the uncertainty of what will "get up" next,
furnishes an amount of excitement which is not to
be found in any other branch of shooting.

If one felt disposed to write a treatise on the
subject, abundance of material presents itself—
Firstly, one might discuss the "head-quarters" to
be selected; secondly, the quantity and quality of
what the Romans so happily termed *impedimenta*,
to be carried; thirdly, the different methods of
"going to work;" fourthly, the various species of
shore birds to be met with, and how to tell them
at a distance, by their actions on the ground, by
their flight, and by their note; fifthly, how to skin
and preserve them if desired; and lastly, how to
cook and eat them.

As to "head-quarters," it is, perhaps, needless
to observe that large and fashionable seaside towns
should be studiously avoided—a small fishing village, near a tidal harbour, with a few scattered
houses and a single inn, is the desideratum. You
may either lodge at the inn, or look out for a more

comfortable room in a neighbouring farmhouse : it is advisable to sleep as near your fishing as possible, to economize time and lessen fatigue.

The amount of luggage you take need not be much—a couple of old shooting suits that are not to be seen again " in society," a pair of waterproof boots for the marsh, a pair of lace-up boots for the punt, with gaiters for the shingle to keep out the stones, a change of linen proportionate to your length of stay in the place, and a few pairs of warm woollen socks, will be amply sufficient for all purposes.

As to guns, an ordinary 12-bore breechloader, with three sizes of shot in the cartridges, will kill anything you are likely to come across, if it be only held straight ; the regular long punt gun, carrying a quarter or half a pound of shot, is all very well for the professional gunner, who has to keep himself and family by the sale of the birds he kills, but it is quite superfluous with the amateur, who, if he is a fair shot, can kill quite as many birds as he requires in a day, especially if he means to preserve them afterwards.

As to the size of shot, opinions differ widely.

An old fowler of our acquaintance says, " Depend
upon it, sir, small shot is the best," and after many
trials we are disposed to agree with him. We have
on many occasions shot all day with No. 7, and
bagged snipe, duck, teal, coots, and water-hens.
But although this size will do very well in the
marsh, where you can walk well up to your birds, it
will not do to trust to it in the punt, where you are
often compelled to fire at long ranges, and consequently require a heavier shot. Do not forget a
waterproof cartridge bag, for nothing is more annoy-
ing than to find after a shower that the cartridges in
your pocket have bulged with the wet and will not
go into the gun. Should this happen at a distance
from home, all sport for the day is at an end. In
addition to the above-mentioned items, it is desirable
to take with you a pocket flask, a bottle or two of the
best pale brandy (never trust to the best " British "
at the inn), a couple of pounds of tea, and, if you
have reason to doubt the quality of the larder, a
tongue, brawn, or what not, to carry you on until
such time as you can stock the larder yourself with
the produce of your gun. Should you forget, or
omit, to take your own tea with you, and find that at

the inn bad, a tablespoonful of good brandy effects a wonderful improvement in it.

As regards the bird-stuffing apparatus, all that you will require will be a sharp knife, a pair of scissors (nail-scissors are best), a supply of cotton wool, a canister of plaster-of-Paris, a tin of arsenical paste, with a brush to use it, needles, thread, and a wooden knitting-needle. With these few items you may skin and preserve anything in the world, as we purpose to show later in a few hints on the subject.

CHAPTER II.

HOW TO GO TO WORK.

ALTHOUGH some few species of shore birds may be found on our coasts throughout the year, the majority of them, and certainly the most attractive species, are birds of double passage ; that is to say, they visit us in flocks in spring on their way northwards to their breeding haunts, and again in autumn on their return southwards for the winter. Thus it will be seen that it is not enough to select a favourable locality for shore shooting, but success will to a certain extent depend upon the time of year at which that locality is visited. May and August are, *par excellence*, the two best months for shore shooting. In May the flocks are composed exclusively of old birds, which have by that time assumed, more or less, their summer plumage ; in August the greater portion of the flocks which visit us consist of young birds in a phase of plumage intermediate in colour between the summer and winter dress of their parents. Heavier bags will be made in autumn than in spring; first, because the flocks which pass southwards in autumn are much larger than those which go northwards in spring; and secondly, because the young birds are less shy and suspicious, and will permit a much nearer approach.

Having arranged these preliminaries, then, the choice of locality and the time to visit it, you arrive at the " happy hunting ground " with the necessaries before referred to. The next question is how to go to work. In the first place, it is necessary to learn the geography of the neighbourhood, and a day or two thus employed will be well spent. It is not to be supposed that this means a walk along shore. We have alluded to the vicinity of a tidal harbour or river mouth. More birds will be found in such situations than along shore, because there is more fresh food to be obtained there. You must visit the harbour, then, at flood-tide and ebb-tide ; ascertain which of the " muds " are last covered by water, and first exposed at the turn of the tide ; and find out whither the birds go at high water. Some birds, as the

Knots, Ringed Plover, and Dunlins, go on to the beach, and doze on the warm shingle till the water falls again ; others, as the Golden Plover, Peewits, and Godwits, betake themselves to the meadows and marshes, and appear to be " on the feed " all day. A good deal of information may be obtained from the native fishermen, and the best plan is not to go down to the beach and engage the first man who offers, for he will probably know less on the subject than any one else, but quietly find out at the inn who has the best reputation for wildfowling, and send for him overnight, when you can arrange plans for the next morning.

There are several ways of getting to birds. You may punt down the harbour at low water, and shoot them on the " muds ; " you may stalk them at high tide under cover of a sea wall, or bank of shingle, or you may " lay up " in their line of flight just before high water, and shoot them as they leave the harbour for the beach or marshes. The last-named plan answers admirably if you happen to select the right spot ; and as soon as the last " mud " is nearly covered, and the birds begin to move, you may have some capital shooting if you only hold straight.

We have frequently had eight or ten birds of various kinds down before we could stop to pick up one, and in consequence have lost many a winged bird, which had time to run and hide before it could be secured. In a case like this a good retriever is invaluable; the plan which ensures the heaviest bag, however, with the least fatigue is undoubtedly the first named. In this case you must start on a flood-tide, a little before high water, and punt down the channels or creeks, which often lie so much below the mud as to prevent your seeing anything as you proceed except a high mud bank on either side of you. If you don't know how to scull, you must take a man with you who does, and who is acquainted, moreover, with the habits of the birds, and knows how to get at them. By "sculling" we do not mean that you are to sit upright, and with a pair of long oars pull and "feather" as on the Cam or Isis, but lying down in the punt with a single short oar in an outrigged rowlock on your right, you propel the punt with a movement analogous to the "screw" of a steamer. It requires some practice to work a punt in this way, especially in difficult channels and shallow water.

We do not here dilate upon the most desirable

form of punt, because, unless you take your own, you must be content with what you can get. Suffice it to say that we do not refer to a fishing-punt with a heavy well and square ends, but to a gunning-punt, narrow, long, and light, decked-in fore and aft, and just big enough to take two persons only. Under the fore-peak you may stow away your cartridges "high and dry," not forgetting flask and sandwiches, besides a good spy-glass and some cotton wool and newspaper for any choice birds that may be worth preserving. Thus equipped you lie down in the bows, with your left arm and head just resting on the fore-deck, and your gun pointing ahead in front of you. Alongside and behind you lies your man, of whom little is to be seen save his right hand upon the oar.

CHAPTER III.

THE BIRDS TO BE MET WITH.

AWAY you go with an easy gliding motion, the water lapping against the flat sides of the punt, till the little fishing village fades behind you in the distance, and you find yourself in a dreary waste of mud and water far from every living thing save the birds whose lives you are intent upon compassing. Foremost amongst these the *inevitable* Dunlins, Oxbirds, or Purres, as they are variously called, will doubtless first attract your attention. These and the Ringed Plovers, from their insignificant size, often escape the fate of their larger congeners, and being unmolested, become emboldened to advance nearer to the houses than any of the others, and thus are generally the first to be met with. Scattered over the mud in little flocks, they may be seen in every variety of attitude, standing, running, flying; now and then a lame one amongst them hopping vigorously on one leg and vainly attempting to keep pace with his more nimble companions. It is well to scan these little flocks with your glass, for now and then a stranger may be detected in the ranks. The Curlew Sandpiper (*Tringa subarquata*), for instance, which resembles the Dunlin at a distance, but which on a nearer view is seen to stand higher on his legs, with a longer body and white upper tail-coverts. In winter, the resemblance is greater than in summer, for at the latter season the plumage of these two species is very different, the Dunlin displaying a black breast, the Curlew Sandpiper having the same part chestnut. A common bird in our harbours generally is the Redshank (*Totanus calidris*) (the fishermen always call them Red-legs), and it is not a difficult species to approach. You may get tolerably close to them sometimes in a punt, and if you can whistle well when "laying up" on shore, you may easily call them within shot. They have a wild, musical note, which harmonizes strangely with the wild wastes over which it is heard. So loud is their call, moreover, that it may be heard long before the birds are in sight. From an observation made in one of the Sussex harbours, we reckoned that the note could be heard at the distance of a mile and a half; for, when "lying up" at the mouth of the harbour, waiting for the flood-tide to take the birds off their legs, we could hear the Redshank's call just about the time that the highest "muds" would be covered, a mile and a half distant. In less than a minute afterwards the birds came in sight—a long, straggling flock; and in less than two minutes three of their number were lying dead at our feet. There is a larger species of Redshank known as the Spotted or Dusky Redshank (*Totanus fuscus*), which is met with, but rarely, in the same situations. Beyond its superior size, it may be readily distinguished by its longer legs and longer bill, the mandibles of which come to a finer point, while the upper mandible hooks over the under to a more noticeable extent. The plumage in winter is not unlike that of the commoner species, but in summer the Dusky Redshank becomes almost uniformly black, while the tail is at all seasons longer and more closely barred.

Less rare than the Dusky Redshank, yet by no

means a common bird, is the Greenshank (*Totanus glottis*).   It is never seen in flocks like the Common Redshank, although it will feed in company with the latter species.   It separates, however, from the others on rising, and being an extremely shy and watchful bird, will frequently give the alarm, and so spoil a good shot, for which you may have worked for half an hour.   Single birds may be whistled round within shot if you remain perfectly still; and this applies more particularly to young birds in the autumn. The Greenshank differs from the Redshank not only in the colour of the legs, which are pea-green, instead of orange-red, but in the shape of the bill, which curves slightly upwards, showing, in this respect, an affinity to the Godwits.   Of the last named we have two species,—the Bar-tailed (*Limosa rufa*), and the Black-tailed Godwit (**Limosa** *melanura*).   The Bar-tailed is by far the commoner of the two, and visits our shores regularly in spring and autumn, often in considerable numbers.   In summer plumage it is a remarkably handsome bird, having the whole of the underparts bright bay, while the back is mottled with various shades of brown and black, the tail barred, and the rump white.   So regularly does this bird make its appearance, that on some parts of the coast the 12th of May is called "godwit day," and all the gunners in the place turn out in full expectation of making a good bag. When the birds first come they are very tame, and you may get within thirty yards of them before they will take wing, but after a few shots have thinned their numbers it is not so easy to approach them. They are such good eating, however, that it is well worth a little trouble to bag a few. The Black-tailed Godwit, although formerly a regular summer migrant, nesting in some parts of the eastern counties, is now generally regarded as an occasional visitant only. It has long ceased to breed here, and can only be looked for with any chance of success at the periods of migration in spring and autumn. It is a much-longer legged bird than the Bar-tailed Godwit, and although it assumes a similar rufous plumage in summer, the bright bay colour never extends below the breast as in the other species. The tail too, instead of being barred, is white, terminated by a broad black band. Another bird which undergoes a similar change of plumage, being red in summer and grey and white in winter, is the Knot (*Tringa canutus*). In the autumn this bird may be

c

seen in large flocks, and is often exceedingly tame. It is one of the easiest birds to decoy by an imitation of its note, and as it is not so fast a flyer as many of the shore birds, it is easily stopped. On one occasion we whistled five Knots right over the punt, and stopped them all before they were out of range. On some parts of the coast the Knot is called the "little plover," perhaps from its rounded head and short bill and legs, which reminds one somewhat of a plover.

On the sand and shingle, but not often on the mud, you will see that handsome little bird, Turnstone (*Strepsilas interpres*). Black, chestnut, and white are its principal colours ; a short horn-coloured bill, and orange legs. In size it is somewhat larger than a Ringed Plover, and has a peculiar twittering note, between a whistle and a chatter, and difficult to describe. It looks very black and white on the wing, in consequence of the dark primaries, broad black gorget, and white underparts. Seldom more than three or four are seen together, although it is sometimes seen feeding with Ringed Plovers, and flying with them when disturbed. In the same way the Knot frequently accompanies the flocks of

Dunlin. That handsome black and white bird, the Oyster-catcher (*Hæmatopus ostralegus*), with its long orange bill and pink legs, is more attractive in appearance than in point of flavour. It cannot be recommended for the table; for, as compared with the Godwits, Greenshank, and Knot, its flesh is decidedly coarse and unpalatable. By some it is called the Sea-pie (from its resemblance in colour to the Magpie), by others the Olive (the derivation of which term is uncertain). The appellation of Oyster-catcher is of course a misnomer, for the bird is utterly incapable of opening "a native." Crabs, whelks, and sand-eels furnish it with food, and it can crush a mussel, and prise a limpet off the rock with comparative ease. But the rock-like shell of an oyster, which defies for a time a well-directed blade of steel, fairly bothers a hungry Oyster-catcher. It is not very often that you can get a shot at one of these birds, unless you come upon them unawares. They are very suspicious, and keep a sharp look-out.

But of all shy birds, commend us to the Curlew. If you can see a Curlew within shot before he sees you, and can stalk and kill him, you may flatter yourself you are not a bad hand at shore shooting.   The young birds in autumn, like those of many other species, are more readily approached and decoyed, but to kill an old Curlew, except by a lucky chance, requires an amount of patience, endurance, and stratagem, that few who have not tried it would credit. We have proved on several occasions, however, that the Curlew depends for safety upon his keen sight, and not upon his sense of smell or hearing.   His clear wild cry of *cour-lieu* must be familiar to all who love a walk along shore. His smaller congener the Whimbrel (*Numenius phœopus*) is not unlike him in appearance and habits.   On the south coast this bird is called the Titterel, from his note.   In many places it is known as the May-bird, from its regular appearance on our shores in the month of May.   The young birds are not bad eating, but neither this species nor the Curlew can be compared for flavour to the smaller sandpipers.   The Common Sandpiper comes down to the coast, but generally keeps to the brackish water, and is never seen right out on the mud, like the Dunlin and other small waders.   In the same way the Green and Wood Sandpipers (*Totanus ochropus* and *glareola*) prefer the marsh, and the neighbourhood of fresh-water pools and streams, and thus are seldom met with by the shore shooter unless he wanders inland to vary his bag. Both these birds rise like snipe, and fly rapidly with many twists and turns. They both " shew the white feather" on their backs, but have a different note, and the Wood Sandpiper looks much lighter in colour, while the other is nearly black. On comparison also it will be found that the Wood Sandpiper has a shorter bill and longer legs than its congener, and the tail is much more barred.

Another bird which is common in most harbours at the seasons we have mentioned, and which ought not to be overlooked, is the Grey Plover (*Squatarola helvetica*). In its summer plumage, it is perhaps unrivalled amongst the shore birds for beauty. The back and wings are boldly chequered with black and white, while the whole of the underparts, from chin to vent, are jet black. In its winter plumage, the Grey Plover might be mistaken for another species, and is, in fact, frequently confounded with the Golden Plover; for after the autumn moult all trace of black disappears, and the whole of the underparts from jet black become pure white. So complete a change is very remarkable, and puzzled the ancient naturalists to such an extent that they made two species out of one in different stages of plumage. This was the case also with the Godwits, Knot, Ruff, and others.

The Grey Plover is larger than the Golden Plover, and though it resembles it in winter, it may readily be distinguished by its small hind toe, which is wanting in the other, and by the colour of the axillary plumes, which are black instead of white. It is an excellent bird for the table, and is well worth the trouble of stalking. It has a peculiarly mournful cry, which cannot fail to attract a musical ear, since it consists of two notes, the second of which, with an *appogiatura*, is a semi-tone only above the first. Indeed he who with a taste for sporting combines a love for music, should not fail to make himself acquainted with the wild notes of the shore birds, for he will thus find another charm in the many attractions of shore shooting.

CHAPTER IV.

DIFFICULTIES AND RESOURCES.

As the sun slowly sets, and evening closes in, two ideas forcibly suggest themselves, namely, that it is becoming too dark to shoot. and that dinner would be very acceptable. A few sandwiches and a flask of sherry can scarcely be considered a meal, at all events by the shore shooter, who has worked hard for ten or twelve hours, but eating is quite a secondary consideration—the excitement of the sport does not allow one to think of it. Nevertheless, you must eat to live, as you would live to shoot, and the day's sport ended, there is nothing for it but to return home. The birds to be preserved, each with a little cotton wool in the mouth to prevent the escape of saliva, which would stain the feathers, and placed head first in a cone of paper (such as the grocers make for sugar) to keep the plumage in order, being stowed carefully away;

larger shot substituted in the gun on the chance of getting a duck or heron on the way home; and the solacing pipe well filled and lit; a satisfactory start is finally effected.

As the punt glides slowly on over an ebb-tide, there is abundant time and abundant matter for the most agreeable reflections. The shore line fades from view; land and water unite, you know not where; sea and sky seem one vast element; the clouds so many islands in an unknown ocean. You gaze and dream, and dream and gaze, until a peculiar grating sound at the bottom of the punt rudely dispels the "sublime," and obtrudes the "ridiculous" fact that you are hard and fast on a mud bank. Did you ever get stuck upon a mud bank with the tide running out? If not, don't, if you can help it. It is anything but amusing, and usually provokes bad language. In this dilemma, if you are a novice at "setting," you will in all probability place your oar too deep, and holding on to save it as the punt glides away, you will slowly but surely go overboard. On the other hand, should you escape such a mischance, you may long try in vain to extricate the punt, and sit and row, and stand and shove, until your patience is exhausted, and your pipe goes out. Perhaps, just as you flatter yourself " she is going," some birds pass overhead within twenty yards of you, and, in attempting to pick up the gun in a hurry, you are again nearly overboard. Of course, they are out of sight before you can fire, and you have the dissatisfaction of knowing that you have just missed " something rare."

These are some of the discomforts of shore shooting (and every sport has its discomforts), but a little practice combined with energy will overcome such trifles as these, and make attendant success seem all the greater.

He who shoots for mere sport, and cares not what becomes of his birds at the end of the day, will in all probability find his evenings at the inn somewhat " slow." Books and periodicals may help to while away a portion of the time, and the fragrant weed may soothe, and seem to drive away fatigue; but after a long day's shooting, and a late dinner, an inclination to doze is almost irresistible.

Not only amusement, however, but a good deal of information may often be obtained from the fishermen and professional gunners in the neighbourhood. There are some, no doubt, who would scout the idea of conversing with such men, and call it lowering and undignified. We cannot regard it in that light. Doubtless, if you associate with them as an equal, frequent the public-house with them, and be hail-fellow-well-met on every occasion, their respect will speedily vanish, and their civility will last only so long as you choose to spend your money amongst them. But no one with any respect for himself would think of pursuing such a course as this, and we are convinced that the gentleman who, in con-versation with his inferiors, speaks and acts as a gentleman, does not lower his own position, but elevates theirs. More than this, he may learn a great deal of them.

Many of these fishermen are observant and intel-ligent men; they are out at all hours, and in all weathers; their particular calling obliges them to rise early, to lay their nets, put down their lobster-pots, or steal a march upon the fowl at daybreak, and they thus acquire an amount of information which often surprises a more highly educated, but less observant, man.

Every naturalist discovers, sooner or later, that
one hour abroad before breakfast is worth half a
dozen afterwards. All nature is then seen to perfection; flowers which close their tender petals at
noon are found at morn in all their beauty, on each
expanded leaf a glistening drop; the birds, which
are silent throughout the heat of the day, pour
forth at early light their loudest melodies; the wild-
fowl are busy feeding on the ooze, and the various
species of shore birds, profiting by the first ebb-tide,
are running here and there over the glistening sands,
gleaning hastily the harvest of the sea.

Listen to the fisherman's account of what he has
seen at daybreak—the peregrine stocking his larder,
the kingfisher stealing the little fish from the
lobster-pots as soon as they are exposed by the
receding tide, the hundreds of gulls hovering round
the herring-nets, "three miles out," the divers, or
"sprat-loons," coming up "all round the boat,"
etc., etc., and if you are not amused and instructed
we are very much mistaken. Listen again to the
honest fowler's account of one or two of his lucky
days—how he marked down some ducks in a "rife"
where he could creep to them, how he peeped

quietly over the bank, and saw them all swimming within thirty yards of him, how he stopped four with one barrel, and knocked down a fifth as it went away; or how he killed the three wild swans last winter in the snow, when the cap snapped twice, and his fingers were so cold he could scarcely feel the trigger. If these stories do not keep you awake, and make you long for morning, to accompany him, you are no true sportsman.

But it will often happen that no such resources are needed; there will, perhaps, be half a dozen birds to skin, which will fully occupy you until bed-time, and he who visits the coast to make himself thoroughly acquainted with the shore birds, and intends to collect and preserve specimens for future study and comparison, must make up his mind to take somewhat less sleep than usual.

CHAPTER V.

DISTINGUISHING CHARACTERS OF THE SHORE BIRDS.

HAVING particularized the species which are included in the general term " shore birds," it may be well to point out the characters by which each may be distinguished. It will require some experience and observation before one can readily name every bird in the list, for some of them are subject to such variation of plumage (according to age and season), that were it not for the possession of specimens in intermediate coloration, the summer and winter plumage of one and the same bird might easily be taken to indicate two distinct species.

It will simplify matters if we divide the entire class into two families, the PLOVERS (*Charadriidæ*), and the SANDPIPERS (*Scolopacidæ*).

The former may be known by their round heads and short bills, and by their having only three toes on each foot, all of which are directed anteriorly. The latter have more elongated heads, longer bills, and four toes on each foot, three in front, and one (more or less rudimentary) behind.

In the Plovers, the length of bill seldom varies in any appreciable degree, but in the Sandpipers it often varies very considerably. This is dependent not only upon age, but also (in some species at least), upon sex, the females almost invariably being the larger birds with longer bills.*

There are two modes of conveying an idea of size, either by comparing the bird to be described with a well-known common species; or by giving the actual measurements of such portions of the anatomy as are found to vary least in their relation to each other, e.g. the bill, wing, and tarsus. The latter mode, for many reasons, is the more preferable, and is accordingly here adopted.

The bill is measured along the upper mandible from the base to the tip. The wing is measured from the carpal joint to the end of the first primary.

* Some interesting remarks on this subject will be found in Mr. Stevenson's "Birds of Norfolk," under the head of "Bar-tailed Godwit," vol. ii. p. 253.

The tarsus is measured from what is commonly, but erroneously, called the knee-joint, to the heel.

In the following descriptions, the *average* measurements only are given in inches and tenths, the decimal system being so extremely simple, and so readily-applicable.*

PLOVERS (*Charadriidæ*).

GOLDEN PLOVER (*Charadrius pluvialis*). Entire length, 11 inches; bill, 1 inch; wing, 7·5; tarsus, 1·5. General colour above, hair-brown, suffused with bright yellow spots; below, pure white. In summer, the underparts more or less suffused with black. Axillaries, at all seasons, white. Legs and toes black.

GREY PLOVER (*Squatarola helvetica*). Entire length, 12 inches; bill, 1·2; wing, 7·5; tarsus, 1·6. General colour above, grey and white; chin, white; breast, dusky; underparts, pure white. In summer, dorsal plumage black and white; underparts, from chin downwards, more or less black. Axillaries, at all seasons, black. Bill, legs and toes,

---

* A foot-rule, divided into inches and tenths, and called "a tenth-rule," may be procured of any mathematical instrument maker for a couple of shillings, and will be found extremely useful.

black. A rudimentary hind toe. Young birds of the year are spotted above with yellow like the Golden Plover, but are distinguishable from that species by the hind toe, and black axillaries.

LAPWING or PEEWIT (*Vanellus cristatus*). Entire length, 12 inches; bill, ·9; wing, 9 in.; tarsus, 1·5. General colour above, bronze-green, with black wings; crown black, with long crest; chin, throat and breast, black; cheeks, white; belly, white; under tail-coverts, chestnut; legs and toes, vinous. Has a short hind toe. In winter, the chin and throat are white.

DOTTEREL (*Eudromias morinellus*). Not strictly a shore bird, but met with on the coast at the migratory periods. Entire length, 9·5 inches; bill, ·6; wing, 6 in.; tarsus, 1·3. General colour above, hair-brown, with buff edges to the secondaries; crown, dark brown, bounded by white; throat, white; breast, greyish-brown; belly, chestnut terminated by black, then white. The young have no chestnut or black on the belly. Legs and toes, pale olive-green; soles, yellow-ochre.

RINGED PLOVER (*Ægialites hiaticula*). Entire length, 7·75 inches; bill, ·5 in.; wing, 5·3; tarsus, ·9. General colour above, hair-brown; bill black, base of ditto, yellow; forehead white, with black band above; cheeks, black; chin and upper collar, white; breast and lower collar, black; rest of underparts, white. The shafts of all the quill-feathers medially white. Outer tail-feather on each side white. Legs and toes orange.

LITTLE RINGED PLOVER (*Ægialites minor*). Entire length, 6·25 inches; bill, ·4; wing, 4·5; tarsus, ·8. General colour as in the last named. Distinguished by its smaller size; the shaft of only the first quill-feather white; the rest dusky; and on the inner web of the outer tail-feather, a dark spot.

The young of both species are brown where their parents are black.

KENTISH PLOVER (*Ægialites cantianus*). Entire length, 7 inches; bill, ·5 in.; wing, 4·3; tarsus, ·9. General colour as in the two last named, but distinguished by sandy crown (in the male), by the black collar not meeting on the breast, and by the legs and toes being black instead of yellow.

SANDERLING (*Calidris arenaria*). Entire length, 8 inches; bill, ·9; wing, 5 in.; tarsus, 1 in. General colour in summer, reddish-brown, black and grey above; chin and breast, do.; from breast downwards, pure white. In winter, grey and white above; from chin to vent, pure white; bill, legs and toes, black. Bill as in the Sandpipers.

Note.—Toes three, as in the Plovers.

TURNSTONE (*Strepsilas interpres*). Entire length, 9·5 inches; bill, ·9 in. ; wing, 6 in. ; tarsus, ·9. General colour above, black and chestnut; below, breast black, belly white. Legs and toes orange-red. A small hind toe. The young have no chestnut on the back, but are mottled with black and light brown. At all seasons the rump is white, crossed by a band of black, and the tail black.

OYSTER-CATCHER (*Hæmatopus ostralegus*). Entire length, 16 inches; bill, 2·5 in. ; wing, 10 in. ; tarsus, 1·8 in. General colour above, black, with a white speculum on the wing; head and neck, black; underparts, pure white; bill, orange ; legs and toes, flesh-colour. In winter, the neck becomes white.

SANDPIPERS (*Scolopacidæ.*)

CURLEW (*Numenius arquatus*). Entire length, male 21 inches—female 26 inches ; bill, 5 to 6 in.; wing, 11·5 to 12·25 ; tarsus, 3. General colour above, greyish-brown, with dark centres to each feather; below, breast and flanks, spotted; belly, white; bill, horn-colour; base of under mandible, flesh-colour; legs and toes, lead colour.

WHIMBREL (*Numenius phœopus*). Entire length, male 16 inches—female, 18 inches; bill, 3 to 3·5 inches; wing, 9·5; tarsus, 2 in. General colour similar to the last named, but the axillaries are much more barred, and upon the crown there are two broad bars of brown nearly parallel, extending from the base of the bill backwards to the nape.

COMMON REDSHANK (*Totanus calidris*). Entire length, 11 inches; bill, 1·6; wing, 6·5; tarsus, 1·75; bare part of tibia, ·9. General colour in summer, above, hair-brown, transversely barred with a darker shade; below, white, streaked longitudinally with dark brown; tail, white, barred with dark brown; bill, horn-colour, orange at base; legs and toes, orange. In winter, the plumage is more or less of a uniform grey above, throat dusky, under-parts pure white, legs and toes paler than in summer. The birds of the year are intermediate in colour between the summer and winter plumages of their parents.

SPOTTED REDSHANK (*Totanus fuscus*). Entire length, 12·5 inches; bill, 2·3 ; wing, 6·75 ; tarsus, 2·25; bare part of tibia, 1·5. General colour in summer, sooty black, with a few of the feathers margined and spotted with white ; belly and rump, more or less white; tail, closely barred; bill, horn-colour, the base orange ; legs and toes, vinous. In winter, the plumage above is more or less of a uniform grey, the throat faintly spotted, and the breast and belly pure white. Legs and toes lemon-colour. Birds of the year have the upper portion of the plumage sooty brown, minutely freckled with white ; the whole of the underparts, from chin to vent, white, closely freckled with light ash.

Note.—The tarsus and tibia are much longer than in the Common Redshank, and the bill is not only much longer, but also more attenuated towards the extremity, and the upper mandible curves down-wards at the tip.

COMMON SANDPIPER (*Totanus hypoleucus*). Entire length, 7·5 inches ; bill, 1 ; wing, 4·25 ; tarsus, ·9. General colour above, bronze ; throat, longitudinally streaked with hair-brown. Breast and belly, pure white. Bill, horn-colour, the base, flesh-colour. Legs and toes, greyish-green.

GREEN SANDPIPER (*Totanus ochropus*). Entire length, 9·5 inches; bill, 1·2; wing, 5·5; tarsus, 1·25; bare part of tibia, ·7 in. General colour above, greenish-brown; in summer minutely freckled with white, in winter almost uniform. Below, throat white, longitudinally streaked with dark brown; breast and belly, white; rump, white. Tail, with outer feathers, white; centre feathers broadly barred with black. Bill, slate-colour. Legs and toes, greyish-green.

Note.—This bird has a very peculiar musky smell, somewhat akin to that of the Petrels.

WOOD SANDPIPER (*Totanus glarcola*). Entire length, 9 inches; bill, 1 in.; wing, 5 in.; tarsus, 1·4; bare part of tibia, ·8. General colour, similar to the last named, from which it differs in having a shorter bill and longer legs, all the feathers in the tail barred, and the quill of the first primary white. In the Green Sandpiper all the quills are black.

GREENSHANK (*Totanus glottis.*) Entire length, 12 inches; bill, 2; wing, 7; tarsus, 2·25. General colour, in summer, grey mottled with black; rump, white; wings, black; the shaft of the first primary, white; chin, throat and breast, white, longitudinally streaked with black; belly, pure white. Bill, slate-colour; legs and toes, pale green. In winter, all trace of black disappears from the upper portion of the plumage; and the whole of the underparts, from chin to vent, are pure white.

Note the form of the bill in this bird. It curves slightly upwards, as in the Godwits, and in this respect connects these birds with the *Totani*.

BAR-TAILED GODWIT (*Limosa rufa*). Entire length, 15 inches; bill, 3·25; wing, 8·5; tarsus, 1·75; bare part of tibia, ·75. General colour, in summer, dorsal plumage, mottled with black and chestnut; wings, black, with white quills; rump, white; tail, barred. Underparts, from chin to vent, uniform chestnut. In winter, the dorsal plumage is mottled with two shades of brown; neck and throat, dusky; breast and belly, white. Bill, horn-colour; base of under mandible, flesh-coloured. Legs and toes, black. Birds of the year somewhat resemble the adult in winter plumage, but have a tinge of buff-colour on the breast and flanks.

Note.—Young birds, whose parents have a distinct summer and winter plumage, exhibit an intermediate phase of colouring the first year.

BLACK-TAILED GODWIT (*Limosa melanura*). Entire length, 16 inches; bill, 3·5; wing, 8; tarsus, 3; bare part of tibia, 1·75. General colour, in summer, head, neck and breast, rufous. Chin, belly and rump, white; dorsal plumage, brown of various shades; primaries, black, with white shafts; tail, black. Bill, pinkish-brown; tip, horn-colour. Legs and toes, dark slate-colour. In winter, all the rufous colouring disappears. The dorsal plumage becomes greyer, the underparts whiter.

Note.—This bird may readily be distinguished from the last named by its superior length of leg and black tail. Moreover, the rufous colouring on the underparts does not extend to the belly, as is the case with the other.

AVOCET (*Recurvirostra avocetta*). Entire length, 16 inches; bill, 3·25; wing, 8·5; tarsus, 3; bare part of tibia, 1·8. General colour, black and white. Crown, nape, scapulars, wing-coverts and primaries, black; the rest of the plumage, white. Bill, black, flattened vertically, attenuated towards the tip, and curved considerably upwards. Legs and toes, pale blue.

BLACK-WINGED STILT (*Himantopus melanopterus*). Entire length, 13 inches; bill, 2·5; wing, 9; tarsus, 4·75; bare part of tibia, 3·3. General colour, black and white. Nape, back and wings, black; the rest of the plumage, white. Bill, black. Legs and toes, pink.

Note.—The rarest of all the British shore birds.

RUFF and REEVE (*Machetes pugnax*). Entire length, male, 12 inches—female, 9 in.; bill, 1·25; wing, male, 7·25—female, 6; tarsus, 1·5.

The colour of this species varies so much in individuals, that it is impossible to describe it in a few words. In summer, the males have the dorsal plumage of all shades of brown, buff, chestnut and purple; on the neck a large ruff or frill (hence the bird's name), of a different colour to the back. Sometimes this frill is of a uniform colour, as chestnut, purplish-black, or white; sometimes it is variegated. It is only assumed during the breeding season, and has entirely disappeared before the shooting season has commenced. In the autumn and winter, the plumage resembles that of the Godwits at the same season; but its smaller size, short and straight bill, and dark rump will always distinguish it. The female, or Reeve, never assumes the frill, but retains much the same colours throughout the year, except that they are much more intense in summer. The colour of the legs and toes varies very much. As a rule, they are lemon-colour or orange. But occasionally one sees a bird with pale green or grey legs.

DUNLIN (*Tringa variabilis*). Entire length, 8 in.; bill, male, 1·3—female, 1·5; wing, 4·5; tarsus, 1. General colour, in summer, head, back and wing-coverts mottled with various shades of brown, black and rufous; on the belly, a patch of black. In winter, the dorsal plumage is, more or less, light brown or grey; the whole of the underparts, pure white. Young birds, in autumn, have the breast and flanks spotted with black. Bill, legs and toes, at all seasons, black.

CURLEW SANDPIPER (*Tringa subarquata*). Entire length, 8·25 inches; bill, 1·5; wing, 5; tarsus, 1·2. General colour, in summer, chestnut, variegated above with black, below with white. Bill, black; slightly curved downwards, like that of a Curlew. Legs and toes, black. In winter, the general colour above is brown and buff; the rump, white; underparts, pure white. Young birds, in autumn, have a tinge of buff on the breast, as remarked in the case of the Godwits.

KNOT (*Tringa canutus*). Entire length, 10 in.; bill, 1·2; wing, 6·5; tarsus, 1·1.

General colour, in summer and winter, like the Curlew Sandpiper and Godwits at the same seasons, except that the rump is variegated, and not white. In summer, the legs and toes are olive, the soles of the feet yellow; in winter they are entirely black.

LITTLE STINT (*Tringa minuta.*) Entire length, 6 inches; bill, ·8; wing, 3·75; tarsus, ·9. Resembles a miniature Dunlin, except that there is never any black on the underparts. In summer, the neck and breast are spotted with rufous, and the dorsal plumage has a large admixture of the same colour. In winter, the spots on the neck and breast disappear, and the dorsal plumage becomes considerably lighter in colour. Bill, legs, and toes at all seasons black.

TEMMINCK'S STINT (*Tringa Temminckii*). Entire length, 5·75; bill, ·6; wing, 3·75; tarsus, ·6. Resembles a miniature Common Sandpiper, and may be distinguished from the Little Stint by its shorter and more slender bill; shorter legs (which are greyish-green instead of black), by its white outer tail-feathers, and by having the shaft of the first primary only white, whereas in the Little Stint all the shafts are white.

PURPLE SANDPIPER (*Tringa maritima*). Entire length, 8·50; bill, 1·4; wing, 5·3; tarsus, 1. The dorsal plumage is purple only in winter. In summer it is variegated with black, brown, and buff, the breast at the same season being spotted. The legs and toes at all seasons are of a yellowish clay colour.

Note.—The colour of the legs (which are very short) will distinguish the bird at all times from any of its congeners.

GREY PHALAROPE (*Phalaropus fulicarius*). Entire length, 8 inches; bill, 1; wing, 5; tarsus, ·8. General colour in summer brown, white, and rufous above; from chin to vent, chestnut. In winter, grey and white above; the underparts pure white. Bill very flat. Feet lobed like a Coot.

Note.—This bird is seldom or never met with in the British Islands in its summer dress. It visits us regularly in autumn (September and October), by which time it has acquired its winter plumage.

RED-NECKED PHALAROPE (*Phalaropus hyperboreus*). Entire length, 7 inches; bill, ·8; wing, 4·5; tarsus, ·8. General colour in summer, black and grey above; on the throat and neck a bright patch of chestnut, underparts pure white. In winter, the rufous colour on the neck disappears, the dorsal plumage becomes much lighter, and the whole of the underparts, from chin to vent, are pure white. The bill is much more slender and pointed than in the Grey Phalarope. The feet are similarly lobed.

Note.—This little bird nests regularly in Scotland and the Hebrides, and visits us in autumn on its way southwards.

It will be observed that the Snipes have been omitted from the foregoing list. They have not been included because it so rarely happens that one meets with a true Snipe on the coast, and because these birds must be too well known to require any description.

In some harbours on the coast where there is a good deal of weed exposed on the mud at low water, we have sometimes met with a Common Snipe in such situations a long way from the shore, but such instances have been rare, and we imagine that Snipe as a rule will always prefer fresh water to salt.

Woodcocks are much more frequently to be met with on the coast, but this is generally after their first arrival, when they alight to rest, or just before their departure in the spring.

Many observers in different parts of the country have witnessed the arrival of Woodcocks in flocks, but we are not aware that these birds have ever been seen to leave the country *in flocks*. Apparently they do not congregate in the spring, but leave our shores singly or in pairs as opportunity and weather may permit.

CHAPTER VI.

ABOUT the end of July, or beginning of August, great numbers of shore birds come into our harbours, and find their way from the mouths of the rivers to a considerable distance inland. Grey Plovers, Godwits, Knots, Whimbrel, Greenshanks, Redshanks, Dunlin, and many other "waders," continue to arrive until the end of August, and the shores and mud-flats which were so deserted during the summer while the birds were away nesting, now present a most animated appearance. Flocks of various species, and of various sizes and colours, from the tiny brown Stint (*Tringa minuta*) to the great grey Heron, are scattered over the ground in all directions; now feeding busily as they follow the receding tide, now flying with noisy call to some more attractive spot. As we look down upon them from the sea-wall, they appear to be all much of the same colour, and are difficult to distinguish upon the brown mud over which they are running. See them in the air with upturned wings, and what a different appearance they present. As the sun strikes upon the pure white of the underparts borne swiftly onwards by rapid wings, the eye is almost dazzled at the bright contrast. Individuals are soon lost to sight as they fly closer together, and the entire flock, gradually lengthening out, sweep across the harbour like a long wave, now light, now dark, as the under or upper portions of the plumage are presented to view. Naturalists who visit the sea-side at the period of migration to which we have alluded, cannot fail to admire the wonderful and graceful evolutions which these birds perform upon the wing; whilst those who reside upon the coast throughout the year must hail with satisfaction the arrival of these feathered strangers, whose presence adds so much to the beauty of the scenery, and relieves, to such an extent, the monotony of sea and sky.

The greater portion of the flocks which visit us in autumn consists of young birds which are on

their way southwards for the winter. The old birds
are seen on their way to the north in May, and after
an absence of six or eight weeks they return with
their young as soon as the latter are able to fly.
The majority of our shore birds annually perform
this double migration; but there are many species
which remain in limited numbers to nest in this
country. Amongst these are the Golden Plover, the
Ringed Plover, the Oyster-catcher, the Common
Sandpiper, the Dunlin, and the Curlew.

The Ringed Plover and the Oyster-catcher remain
near the shore, and lay their eggs upon the sand or
shingle, as the case may be. The Common Sandpiper betakes itself to the north country burnsides,
and generally makes its nest at no great distance
from the water; while the Golden Plover, Dunlin,
and Curlew go on to the moors and peat-bogs, and
bring up their young in the wildest and most unfrequented spots.

When walking over the moors in May we have
repeatedly startled a Curlew from amongst the tall
heather, and have satisfied ourselves on these, as on
other occasions, that this wary bird depends more
upon the sense of sight than hearing to save itself

from its enemies. Ever suspicious, ever on the alert, it is a most difficult bird to stalk unless some good cover intervenes to screen your approach. Now and then upon the coast you may steal a march upon a flock under shelter of a sea-wall; but, as a rule, they keep too far out from the shore to be within reach of a gun from the wall. We have found it a good plan to "lay up" at a spot in the usual line of flight about an hour before high water. As soon as the mud is covered, they leave the harbour, calling loudly at intervals to one another as they fly, and by imitating their call, while lying concealed, we have repeatedly brought a Curlew overhead and within shot. Another plan is to go down the harbour in a gunning-punt, with an ordinary double-gun, at low water, and work along the numerous channels which intersect the great mud-flats. In this way you can often get, unperceived, within shot of a flock of birds, and secure even the wary Curlew.

On one occasion we were lying in a punt in "a drain" (as the small channels in the Sussex harbours are called), a little below a point where another "drain" intersected it almost at right angles. In

the latter we had marked down two Curlews when
several hundred yards off, and observed that they
were feeding towards the junction of the two
" drains." It is always a piece of luck, if birds
feed towards you after you have got as near to them
as you can without alarming them. And this was
the case in the present instance. The Curlews
waded up the side of the drain, which was much
shallower than the one we were lying in, and in
about ten minutes one of them stepped out upon
the flat within twenty yards of the punt, and for a
moment seemed perfectly scared. We at once
cocked the gun and sat up; with a weird scream
the bird took wing, and in another second fell dead
upon the mud. His companion, rising out of the
drain some yards further off, was only winged, and
led us a rare chase over the ooze before he was
secured. This incident shows that the Curlew depends for safety upon his keen sight, and not upon
his power of scent; otherwise the bird in question
would never have walked within a few yards of the
punt, which he could not see until he had stepped
upon the bank.

In the " Zoologist," for 1856, Mr. W. H. Power

has given an account of the way in which the fisher-men at Rainham, in Kent, decoy Curlews within shot. They train a red-coloured dog (as much like a fox as possible) to prowl about and attract the attention of the birds while the gunner lies hidden in a dyke. As soon as the birds chase the dog, which they frequently will do, he draws gradually towards his master, until a shot is obtained. Some-times two or three Curlews are killed at a time in this way; but the plan is said not to answer with a large flock. We can confirm its success, however, with a single bird, for we once killed a Heron which we should probably never have got near, had not a red setter attracted his attention, and on being whistled to, brought up the bird within shot.

Those who have had much experience in shore shooting must have remarked how much Curlews differ from one another in size. Whether this difference is dependent upon age or sex is a point still discussed by naturalists. We have hitherto been inclined to believe that the variation is owing to age; but as this conclusion has been drawn chiefly from external appearances, and in a few instances only from actual dissection (for we generally eat all the Curlews we get); and as in the case of other waders—for example, the Bar-tailed Godwit—the female has proved to be invariably much larger than the male, it is possible that the same rule may hold good with the Curlew.

The note of the Curlew is by far the loudest uttered by any of our grallatorial birds. That observant naturalist William Thompson says, in his "Natural History of Ireland" (Birds, vol. ii. p. 195): " It will perhaps be scarcely credited that it can be heard at the distance of nearly three English miles; yet under peculiar circumstances such is the case. I have heard it so on calm moonlight nights when at the extremity of the bay at Holywood Warren, awaiting the flight of these birds from Harrison's Bay and Conswater, whence the flowing tide would drive them from particular banks respectively two and three miles distant from any station. The call from the first-named locality sounded quite near, and from the latter distinct, though much more faintly; the state of the tide at the time evincing with certainty that all the banks, except the two alluded to, were covered too deeply with water for the birds to be on them. Shore shooters are well aware of this circumstance."

Besides its usual cry of " Cou-r-lieu, cour-lieu," there is another which sounds like " wha-up ;" from which latter cry the bird in Scotland has derived the name of " Whaup ; " and in the spring of the year, when pairing, a softer note is frequently heard, which sounds like " whee-ou, whee-ou."

At one time this bird was a favourite dish with wealthy *gourmands*,* but is now apparently quite out of fashion, except with a few knowing ones at the seaside, and those sportsmen who have proved by experience how good a bird it is when roasted.

The food of the Curlew is very miscellaneous, consisting of all sorts of marine mollusca and crustacea, worms, small fish, and vegetable matter, invariably accompanied with a quantity of sand or small particles of grit. The bird is especially fond of crabs, and we have sometimes killed a Curlew so gorged with crabs and shrimps as to be offensive to the smell and not agreeable as food.

* In the Lord North accounts appears the following item :—
" Kyrlewes to be hadde for my Lordes owne Mees at pryncipall Feestes, and to be at xijd. a pece." Similar items are to be found also in the L'Estrange " Household Book."

Those who are familiar with the works of Professor Wilson must remember his admirable description of the feelings which he experienced when stalking a Curlew.* "At first sight of his long bill aloft above the rushes, we could hear our heart beating quick time in the desert; at the turning of his neck, the body being yet still, our heart ceased to beat altogether—and we grew sick with hope when near enough to see the wild beauty of his eye. Unfolded, like a thought, was then the brown silence of the shy creature's ample wings, and with a warning cry he wheeled away upon the wind, unharmed by our ineffectual hail, seen falling far short of the deceptive distance, while his mate, that had lain crouched—perhaps in her nest of eggs or young, exposed yet hidden—within killing range, half running, half flying, flapped herself into flight, simulating lame leg and wounded wing; and the two disappearing together behind the hills, left us in our vain reason, thwarted by instinct, to resume with live hopes, rising out of the ashes of the dead, our daily disappointed quest over the houseless mosses. Yet now and then to our steady aim the bill of the

* " Recreations of Christopher North."

' Whaup' disgorged blood, and as we felt the
feathers in our hand, and from tip to tip felt the
outstretched wings, fortune, we felt, had no better
boon to bestow, earth no greater triumph." Who
has not at one time or other experienced feelings
such as these, and lacked the power of words to
describe them?

During the winter months, Golden Plovers may
often be found consorting with Peewits and Field-
fares, and feeding on the same diet; but indepen-
dently of their size, they may always be distinguished when on the ground at a distance by their
peculiar motion, running with short quick steps
and stopping abruptly ; now and then dipping down
the head to seize a worm, and elevating the tail considerably.

In enclosed districts they are generally to be
found on the fallows, where they devour large quan-
tities of earthworms; but they are particularly
partial to flooded meadows and the soft ooze of
our tidal harbours. In the meadows they find
abundance of insect and vegetable food; on the
ooze their diet consists chiefly of small mollusca
of various kinds and the fry of the common mussel.

At the approach of rain the flocks become very restless, wheeling about to and fro, and constantly shifting their ground. On this account it is said that the specific name of *pluvialis* has been applied to the bird ; and, in some parts of the country, where it is common, persons profess to foretell the weather by watching the movements of the flocks. So long as the weather remains fine and open, these birds are uncommonly wary; but a dull rainy day seems to take away all their energy, and they sit huddled together, with their heads drawn in between their shoulders, looking, at a little distance, more like inanimate clods of earth than birds. As on these occasions they are more easily approached, the most successful shots we ever made at Golden Plover were always obtained on a wet day; and it would seem, therefore, as if there were good reason for the saying that the bird is called *pluvier* in France : " Parce-qu'on le prend mieux en temps pluvieux qu'en nulle autre saison."

" There is, in shooting Plover, a common remark made by sportsmen, that the *second* is always the most productive barrel. The rapidity with which they vary their position when on the ground seldom admits of a grand combination for a sitting, or rather a running, shot. But, when on the wing, their mode of flight is most favourable for permitting the shot to tell; and it is by no means unusual to bring down a number. When disturbed, they frequently wheel back directly above the fowler, and offer a tempting mark, if he should have a barrel in reserve. And even when too high for the shot to take effect, I have often thrown away a random fire; for the Plover, on hearing the report, directly make a sweep downwards on the wing; and I have, by this means, brought them within range of the second barrel."*

Thompson, in referring to this singular habit of the Golden Plover,† gives an amusing anecdote on the subject, as related to him by a friend.

" In the winter of 1847, I went to some boggy meadows in the neighbourhood of Belfast, for the purpose of shooting Golden Plover, and took with me a young lad who had never before been on such an expedition. When returning home, a flock, consisting of about fifty, of these birds flew over-

* " Wild Sports of the West," p. 292.
† "Nat. Hist. of Ireland,"—Birds, ii. p. 88.

head, beyond reach of the shot ; but, as I despaired
of getting nearer to them, I fired at the flock, on
which they instantly swept down, almost perpen-
dicularly, within three or four yards of the ground.
My companion ran forward, in the greatest delight,
to pick up, as he expected, the entire flock ; when,
to his utter amazement, they all resumed their
former mode of flight, and quickly disappeared in
the distance."

Towards the end of March, or beginning of April,
the large flocks break up ; and smaller parties may
be observed moving northwards again, towards their
breeding haunts. About this time, sundry black
feathers make their appearance on the throat and
breast, giving indications of that remarkable change
from winter to summer plumage, when the under
parts, from being pure white, become jet-black.

We shall not easily forget the first occasion on
which we met with the Golden Plover in summer
plumage.

Walking, in the middle of May, over a wild moor
in Northumberland, where the eye rested on nothing
but heather and sky, we were watching the circling
flight of a Curlew, and wondering whether we could

find the nest. Suddenly, we were almost startled by a soft clear whistle, which sounded so close at hand, that we turned round, expecting to find a follower who might have some message to deliver. Nothing was to be seen; and while we gazed and wondered, again it sounded clear and plaintive, bringing to mind those lines of Walter Scott, in the " Lady of the Lake":—

> " And in the Plover's shrilly strain,
> The signal whistle's heard again."

There was something very ventriloquial in the sound; and it was a long time before we were able to determine the exact direction whence it proceeded.

At length, having decided this, and concluding that it must be a Golden Plover, although the note differed from the well-known call which we had so often heard in winter, we went down on hands and knees and crawled stealthily towards the spot where we supposed the bird to be, stopping, now and then, to listen for the guiding call.

So fully convinced were we that the bird was at least a hundred yards ahead, that it was with considerable surprise we came upon it before we had accomplished half that distance.

We can conceive few emotions more pleasurable
than that which sways the mind of a naturalist
when looking upon a species which is new to him;
and we shall never forget the delight which we
experienced on that occasion, when, peering through
the heather, we saw, for the first time, within ten
yards of us, a black-breasted Golden Plover. Although so many years ago, we can still recall every
attitude of the bird as we first saw it. The uplifted
wing and short quick run, as if for a meditated
flight; and then the sudden repose and motionless
attitude, on finding that no danger threatened. We
watched it till our eyes swam, when another came
in view, announcing its presence by a soft whistle,
exactly similar to that we had heard before.

Our curiosity satisfied, we rose to our feet, and
both birds took wing. Soon we saw a third, and a
fourth; and, picking up the almost forgotten gun,
began to think of securing one or two specimens for
closer examination. This we had no difficulty in
doing, for the birds were by no means wild. We
concluded from their actions, and from the early
date, that they had not yet commenced to nest; and
this conclusion was strengthened by the fact that

we searched a large tract of ground for more than three hours without finding any eggs.

The two specimens which we carried home had not quite assumed their full summer dress, there being still a few white feathers cropping out upon the breast and belly. The stomachs of both contained a number of little shining beetles, and a few small univalves, of which we could not then determine the species.

Had we remained later on the moor referred to, we should, in all probability, have been rewarded by finding the eggs, since we have been assured that the Golden Plover breeds there annually. The nest is a very slight affair, not unlike that of the Peewit; and the eggs, also, are very similar to the Peewit's eggs, although larger and more richly coloured.

The young, when first hatched, are remarkably pretty little things, being powdered over, as it were, with golden yellow, upon a brown and grey ground-colour. They run as soon as they leave the shell, and fly well by the end of July. The family parties then unite in August, and begin to form those dense flocks to which we have already referred, and which

are looked for, in winter, with such eagerness by
sportsmen in the south.

The Peewit may be considered a resident species,
for it may be found in some part or other of the
country all the year round. There is no doubt that
great numbers move southwards at the approach
of winter; and the birds which we notice in the
southern counties in the fall of the year, are probably visitors from more northern localities.

In many parts of the country we have remarked
that the same ground is annually resorted to by
Peewits for the purpose of nesting; and hence we
may conclude that the same birds return year by
year, impelled by curious instinct, to the very spot
where they have formerly reared their young. They
pair towards the end of March, and early in April
collect straws and dry grass, and form a slight nest
in a depression of the ground. When the full com-
plement of eggs is laid, each nest contains four, and
the harvest time for poulterers and game-dealers
commences about the middle of April. When the
locality which the birds have selected has been dis-
covered, dozens of eggs may be picked up on a few
acres, for Peewits are gregarious in their habits,

and the nests are frequently only a few yards apart. The eggs, which are considerably pointed at the smaller end, seldom vary much in colour, being olive-brown, spotted and splashed towards the larger end with black or dark umber. We have once or twice taken eggs of this species which were of a pale stone-colour, with small black spots at the larger end. These strikingly resemble very large eggs of the Ringed Plover (*Charadrius hiaticula*), and afford an illustration of the fact that some birds, while usually laying eggs peculiar in colour to their own species, occasionally lay eggs which resemble those of other species in the same family. We have noticed this in many cases.

The young Peewits are very active as soon as they are hatched; and as they leave the nest at the approach of an enemy and cower down close to the ground, the mottled brown colour of their backs renders it very difficult to catch sight of them in this position. In this way, no doubt, they often escape destruction.

The food of the Peewit is, to a great extent, insectivorous. The stomachs of a great many of these birds, which we have shot and examined on

grass-land upon a clay soil, were filled with different
species of small *Coleoptera*, and minute particles of
grit, while others, which we procured on down-land
upon a chalk soil, contained fragments of two *Mollusca* which are extremely common in such situations,
—*Helix virgata* and *Helix caperata*. It is the *Helix
caperata*, by the way, which, being taken up with
grass by sheep, is said to impart the excellent
flavour to the South-down mutton. Judging by the
condition of the Peewits which had fed upon this
mollusk, we should say that its properties are very
fattening.

When the birds get down to the shore, they lose
their flavour, and are then not nearly so good for the
table. We have noticed this in the case of the
Curlew, Golden Plover, Grey Plover, Redshank,
and many others, besides the Lapwing. The reason
of this, no doubt, is the change in their diet. On
the shore they get sand-hoppers, shrimps, and other
small *Crustacea*, which impart more or less a marine
and disagreeable flavour.

As the name "Peewit" has been given to the bird
from its peculiar note, so has the name "Lapwing"
reference to its characteristic flight.

Those who live in the country must have noticed how appropriately both these names have been applied. In some places the bird is known as the " Green Plover " in spring, and the " Black Plover " in winter. At the approach of the nesting season the back and scapulars become of a dark but bright metallic-green colour. In the winter this colour becomes darker and duller, until at a little distance it looks almost black.

On most parts of the coast the Heron may be seen at low water, fishing in the little pools which have been left by the receding tide; here he finds crabs, shrimps, and other delicacies; but instead of being sociable, like the Gulls and Redshanks, and inviting a friend to join him at dinner, he goes to his own particular pool, like an old gourmand to his club, and keeps the best of everything to himself.

We have watched him on the rocky weed-covered shore of Northumberland, on the shining sands of Lancashire, and on the dreary mud-flats of the Sussex harbours, and have found him always the same; shy and suspicious, even where seldom disturbed, he seems to have a wonderful eye to danger, and, we almost believe, can distinguish a gun from a stick or an umbrella.

Now and then, upon a rocky coast, we have stalked him under cover of a friendly boulder, and while our heart beat loud with the rapid exertion and excitement, we have shot him just as he had detected our head above the rock. And what a triumph we have felt in standing over his prostrate form, and smoothing his expansive wings, feeling in that moment a sufficient reward for having crawled, on hands and knees, perhaps three hundred yards of trea-cherous ground, slipping over sea-weed, and through salt-water pools. But it was never thus on the mud-flats; there no friendly barrier intervened to screen our approach, and we could only advance near enough to be just out of shot, when the large wings were unfolded, and we were left to stand and gaze wistfully after the coveted prize. Now and then at early dawn, we have come suddenly upon a Heron while busily employed under the steep bank of a brook, and have thus been enabled to knock him down with Snipe shot before he could get out of range. It was ludicrous to observe the surprise of the bird when he first became aware of our

presence, and with a hoarse croak clumsily endeavoured to get away. On one occasion, accompanied
by a red setter, we were stalking a Heron, when
the dog, over-anxious, ran forward and attracted the
attention of the bird, which immediately took wing;
instead of flying away, however, he hovered over
the dog, looking down at him like a hawk. We
crouched down and gave a low whistle, and the
dog coming back, actually brought up the Heron
within shot, when we fired and killed him. The
bird seemed to follow every movement of the dog,
and was so intently eyeing him, that he never saw
us until the gun was raised; he then turned at once
to make off, but too late.

On the coast, the Heron feeds at low water during
the day, and in unfrequented marshes he may also
be caught fishing in broad daylight; but when
compelled to get his living at reservoirs, ponds,
and rivers, which are oftener visited by his enemy,
man, he prefers to come just before daybreak or
after dusk. In autumn, when the brooks run dry,
we have frequently noticed the impressions of his
long toes, visible for miles on the soft mud, showing
the great extent of ground traversed in his patient

search for food. Fish, frogs, mussels, and even water-rats, are all included in the Heron's bill of fare. He will take young water-fowl, too, from the nest, and after pinching them all over in his formidable bill, and holding them under water till they have become well saturated, he throws up his head, opens his mandibles, and the " Poule d'eau souché " disappears.

Some years ago we paid a visit, in the month of May, to a certain reservoir in Yorkshire, where the Pochard (*Anas ferina*) was known to have bred, our object being to ascertain whether this duck was then nesting there, and to learn what other fowl were on the water. We might say a good deal of that pleasant excursion, but must confine our attention for the present to the Heron. At one end of the reservoir is, or was, a thick bed of willows, extending out some distance from the shore. The water at this spot is shallow, with a muddy bottom. Coots and Moorhens were numerous and noisy, swimming about amongst the willows, and collecting materials for their nests. We lay upon the grass at the edge of the water, peering quietly through the willows, and learnt a good deal of the private life of these water-fowl. While we were gazing, a Heron, which must have flown unnoticed up the water, dropped suddenly in the shallow, within twenty yards of our ambush. Here was an opportunity for observation : scarcely venturing to breathe, we watched with interest every motion of the great grey bird. His long black crest and pendent breast feathers showed him to be fully adult, and we thought at the time we had seldom seen a Heron in finer plumage. With head and neck erect, he took a cautious glance all round, as if to satisfy himself that he was unobserved, and apparently assured, he then looked down at the water; for some minutes he never altered his position, till at length, bending slowly and gracefully forward, he suddenly struck the water with his bill, and recovered a small fish. A pinch, a toss of the head, and it had disappeared down his throat. He then drew himself together with apparent satisfaction, wiped his bill upon his long breast plumes, and, slightly altering his position, prepared, as an angler would say, to make another " cast." At this moment, we incautiously moved a little to one side to avoid a willow bough and obtain a better view, when his quick eye instantly detected the movement, and in another second he was flying down the water in the direction whence he had come.

There are few sights more gratifying to a naturalist than a heronry. We have had the privilege of visiting three : one at Walton Hall, Yorkshire, the seat of the late Charles Waterton ; one at Milton, near Peterborough, belonging to the Hon. George Fitzwilliam ; and one at Wanstead, the property of Lord Cowley. Did space permit, we might give a detailed and interesting account of all we saw on these occasions, but we can do no more than offer a few brief remarks on the general appearance and situation of the heronry last named.

The date of our visit was the 5th of April, and the birds were then sitting on their eggs. The Heron is one of the few waders which resort to a tree for the purpose of nidification, and a stranger sight than a number of these great birds, perched at the top of a lofty elm, can scarcely be imagined. Twenty years ago, the Herons at Wanstead Park tenanted some trees at a different spot to that which they now frequent. At present they occupy some tall elms upon an island in the largest piece of water in the park. The keeper informed us that there were about thirty pairs. We proceeded to the boat-house, and after baling out the boat, which was nearly full of water, steered for the Herons' island. A good glass enabled us to see the birds very clearly, and most of them were in splendid plumage. The nests were placed at the very tops of the trees, and many of them were occupied by a sitting bird.

Here and there a Heron stood erect upon a bough, with head and neck drawn in, looking for all the world like a cold sentinel, with his bayonet between his teeth, and his hands in his trousers' pockets. As we approached the island several loud croaks were heard, and the sentinels took wing, the sitting birds being the last to leave. Taking it for granted that the bird which sat the longest was the most likely to have eggs, we selected a tree from which a Heron flew as we reached it.

It was a wych-elm about forty feet high, and the nest was placed amongst the topmost branches. After a fatiguing climb, owing to the absence of boughs for a considerable distance, we reached the top, and paused to rest before looking into the nest. And now was the anxious moment. Were our exertions in vain? Was the nest empty, or were we to be rewarded with the sight of eggs? The nest was large enough to sit in, composed externally of large twigs, chiefly elm and willow, and lined with smaller twigs, fibre and dry grass. It overhung our head to some extent, so that we were obliged to pull away a portion of the side before we could see into it, when, to our delight, four beautiful eggs were displayed, their bright bluishgreen colour contrasting well with the dark fibre on which they were laid.

The wind blew in gusts, and it was no easy matter to get them down safely; but at length we succeeded in getting them into our handkerchief, and holding the ends together in our mouth, brought them down without a crack. They were considerably incubated, showing that they had probably been laid about the end of the third week in March. The Heron, indeed, is one of the earliest birds to breed. The young, when first hatched, present a very remarkable appearance, and are fed by their parents for a long time before they can shift for themselves.

A friend once kept a Heron on his lawn, and a

very amusing bird he was. When first captured, he was very sulky, and refused all food. Fearing he would starve, the owner forced some fish down the bird's throat, but the next moment saw it returned upon the grass. The process was repeated with the same result, and a third time my friend endeavoured ineffectually to overcome the obstinacy of his captive. At length, reflecting how the Chinese treat their tame Cormorants, by fastening a strap round the neck to prevent the fish from *going down*, he tied a piece of tape round the Heron's neck, to prevent the fish, in this case, from *coming up*. The experiment was perfectly successful, and the bird, finding it impossible to disgorge, at length abandoned the attempt, and subsequently fed himself. Fish were placed for him in a fountain on the lawn, and he evinced great delight in taking them from the water. One day a rat was observed helping himself to the Heron's food. The rightful owner caught him in the act, and with one blow of his formidable bill felled him to the ground. Seizing him, then, before he could recover, he carried him squeaking to the fountain and ducked him. After shaking him well under water, he held him up for examination. The rat spluttered and squeaked in abject terror, and again was he submerged. The dose was repeated, until the unfortunate rat at length succumbed, and being by this time nice and tender, the Heron pouched him, and his then elongated form was seen distending the thin skin of the bird's neck in its passage downwards, until it finally disappeared for ever.

A singular bird is the Ruff. Belonging to the same great group which comprises the Snipes and Sandpipers (*Scolopax, Tringa* and *Totanus*), it differs remarkably from them all in many respects. Old naturalists placed it among the *Tringæ*, but as the species became better known, it was found that, unlike any other wading bird, the males are polygamous, and fight for possession of the females; they differ from each other in colour; are a third larger than their mates; and during the breeding season put forth a curious frill of feathers on the neck, which disappears in autumn, when the sexes separate. These facts led naturalists to consider the bird *generically* distinct from those above named, and it is now usually placed in the genus *Machetes,* which Cuvier, in 1817, proposed for it.

By far the most complete account which has been given of the Ruff and Reeve is that which was published by Montagu, in 1813, in the supplement to his " Ornithological Dictionary." This distinguished naturalist travelled from Devonshire into Lincolnshire—a long journey in those days—with the sole object of studying these birds in their native fens, and of ascertaining more than was then known of their habits and curious change of plumage. He experienced the greatest difficulty in discovering the haunts of these birds, for the fen-men, who made a business of snaring them for the table, refused to give him any information on the subject, fearing lest their trade might be interfered with. He attained his object, nevertheless, and carried back with him several live Ruffs to Devonshire. These he kept in confinement for a few years, and carefully noted all the changes of plumage which they underwent, and the peculiarities of habit which they displayed. His interesting remarks on the subject should be read *in extenso* by every naturalist.

The male birds, as the name *Machetes* implies, are extremely pugnacious, and this is especially the case at the commencement of the breeding season when the birds are pairing. Two Ruffs will then contend for the possession of a Reeve, and with heads lowered, frill distended, and wings trailing the ground, they rush at one another again and again, like game-cocks, leaping and striking with the bill, until one or other is forced to yield. Having paired and selected a spot for the nest, they build not unlike a Snipe, and in much the same situations, generally choosing the middle of a tussock or clump of sedge. Here they lay four eggs of an oil-green colour, blotched chiefly at the larger end with liver brown.

It is remarkable that one seldom sees two Ruffs of the same colour; the variety is surprising. As a rule, the male bird renews the same coloured frill in each succeeding year. This has been proved repeatedly by marking birds in confinement and noting their changes of plumage; but it has occasionally happened that a Ruff which had a light frill one year, assumed one of a darker shade the succeeding spring. The frill begins to make its appearance in April, and before the end of July it has almost disappeared.

The breeding haunts of this bird in England have

been unfortunately almost destroyed. Mr. Stevenson says that in East Norfolk a few pairs still nest annually, and are strictly preserved. In Suffolk, Cambridgeshire, and Yorkshire, where this species was once plentiful, it has now ceased to breed, and in the more northern counties of Durham and Northumberland a nest is very rarely found. We have lately been informed that a few pairs have been found nesting in Lincolnshire within the last two years.

During the months of August and September, at which season great numbers of shore birds migrate southwards, the Ruff and Reeve are more commonly met with. We have found them at this time of year in the tidal harbours on the east and south coasts, and have several times shot them when looking for Snipe in marshy ground near the sea. The males had then lost their frills, and were only to be distinguished from the females by their larger size and darker plumage. The colour of the legs varies almost as much as the colour of the frills. Orange, lemon, clay colour, lead colour, and black may be found, with all the intervening shades, and this difference of colour in the legs as well as in the plumage led some of the older naturalists to create some confusion by describing different individuals as distinct species.

The practice of netting birds for the table in the spring of the year, after the pairing has commenced, is most reprehensible. To destroy the breeding-grounds, and kill the old birds, is a sure way to make a species extinct, and yet this is what is being done in the case of the Ruff and Reeve. We would earnestly beg of those who may meet with these birds in suitable localities for nesting, in the spring of the year, to leave them unmolested, and not to cause another name to be added to the list of beautiful creatures which have already become extinct as residents in this country.

CHAPTER VII.

ON SKINNING AND PRESERVING BIRDS.

We have frequently heard sportsmen regret that for want of a knowledge of taxidermy they have been prevented from preserving many a beautiful bird which had fallen to the gun, and which they would have given anything to keep. Undoubtedly, the art of bird-preserving is best learnt by watching the operations of an experienced hand; failing this, a few simple directions, carefully read over and faithfully followed, ought to enable one to master the rudiments. Practice will ensure perfection.

For the benefit, then, of those who may be anxious to learn, we propose to bring our remarks to a close with a few practical hints on the subject, taking nothing for granted, and assuming no previous knowledge on the part of the reader, except an acquaintance with the terms generally employed to designate the various portions of the animal frame.

When discussing in Chapter I. the items of luggage which ought to be packed up for such an excursion, attention was directed to the bird-stuffing apparatus. The necessary materials may be here recapitulated. A sharp knife, a pair of nail-scissors, some cotton wool, plaster-of-Paris, arsenical paste and brush, needles, thread, and a wooden knitting-needle. We will suppose that the bird to be preserved is a Grey Plover (*Squatarola helvetica*), in the handsome black and white plumage which is assumed in the spring. You have already (so soon as it was shot) put some cotton wool in the mouth and placed it in a cone of paper, for reasons above mentioned. Remove this wool, now saturated and stained with saliva; substitute a fresh bit; tie up the bill, preventing the thread from slipping by passing it through the nostril. Lay the bird on its back; break the *humerus* on each side; the wings will then lie open and be out of the way. Part the feathers on the breast, and with the nail-scissors cut the skin down to the vent. Pick up the edge of the skin on one side with the nail of the left forefinger; hold it between that finger and the thumb; and with the knife in the right hand separate the skin from the body as far as possible both ways until the leg and wing, or rather portions of them, the *femur* and *humerus*, on that side, are exposed. Throw in some plaster-of-Paris and rub it gently against the skin, to absorb the moisture, and to prevent any blood or grease that there may be from soiling the feathers. Take hold of the *femur* with the left forefinger and thumb; press the right forefinger and thumb against the skin and close to the *tibia;* then draw the latter out of the skin for half its length; break it across the middle, and with the scissors cut through the flesh and ligaments which surround the bone. Take hold of the foot and draw it towards you, when one half of the *tibia* will return to its place, the other half remaining attached to the body, which may then be further skinned on that side as far as the caudal vertebræ. Proceed in the same way with the other side, and now having got both legs free, and the skin below them adhering only round the caudal vertebræ, turn the bird over, breast downwards, and head towards you. Pressing your left thumb upon the tail-coverts and drawing the skin back towards you as far as it will come, the body is pushed outwards in a semicircular form, the concavity towards you. With the knife, or scissors, the caudal verte-

G

brae must then be severed as near the tail as possible. Next take the body with a firm grip in your left hand, and holding it just above the thighs, push the skin gently off the back until you reach the wings, using a little plaster as you proceed. Draw out the *humerus* on one side (already broken) until the splintered end appears. Cut away the flesh and ligaments surrounding the bone, and one wing will then be free. Proceed in the same way with the other wing, and the whole of the body will then be skinned, except the neck and head.

The skin will now be inside out. Separate the body from the head, leaving the neck attached to the latter to enable you to hold it with the left hand, while with the right you push the skin down over the head until the cranium is fairly exposed to view. With the sharp points of the scissors cut out the roots, so to say, of the ears, otherwise in trying to remove the skin you will tear it. In the same way cut the membrane which connects the eyelids with the orbits, and you will thus avoid tearing the former. Having then skinned the head right down to the base of the bill, cut away not only the neck but a sufficient portion of the occiput, to admit of the brain being extracted. Remove the tongue and palate, and with these the piece of cotton wool which was placed in the mouth at starting. You have now nothing but the bare skin turned inside out, with a portion only of the wings and legs remaining in their places, and the reduced portion of the cranium as clean as may be. This will be the best time for removing all particles of fat and flesh which may still be adhering to the skin, and for drying the skin as much as possible with plaster-of-Paris, which, however, must not be allowed to remain, but must be brushed off with a little cotton wool. Dipping your brush in water, you will now moisten the arsenical paste, giving a very thin coat of it to the skull or what remains of it, and to the inside of the skin of the neck. Fill up the orbits and the mouth with cotton wool, taking care to restore in this way the shape of the head as nearly as may be. Turn the skin, then, back over the head, and proceed to turn the skin of the neck until the extremity of the bill appears. Take hold of the bill in the left hand, and draw the skin gently downwards until it is restored to its proper position. It will then be found that the

feathers of the head, and particularly those around
the eyes, are all awry. Here the wooden knitting-
needle will prove useful. By inserting it through
the eyelids, the skin can be raised and depressed at
any particular point, and the feathers consequently
made to lie in their natural order. If it be found
that the head has not been sufficiently stuffed, more
cotton can be introduced through the eye. The skin
being now in order, and the head finished, the
wings next claim attention. Take the broken
humerus between the finger and thumb of the left
hand, and with the right thumb-nail push down the
skin from the *radius* and *ulna* as far as the carpal
joint. Remove all flesh and ligament, apply a little
arsenical paste, wrap the bones round with cotton
wool, and draw back the skin over them, amputating
the *humerus* at the joint. The same with the other
wing ; the same with each leg. Remove any of the
caudal vertebræ that may remain, together with any
flesh and fat that may still be adhering towards the tail.

Now to make an artificial neck, tie the wings, fill
the body, sew it up, and the skin will be completed ;
a good neck may be made of wool wound round the
knitting-needle ; smear it with the arsenical paste,

and insert it with a corkscrew movement into the skin of the neck, until you feel that the point of the needle has touched the base of the skull; reverse the corkscrew movement, and the needle will come away, leaving the wool in the neck; bring the wing-bones to the centre of the skin, and tie them together, not quite close, but just enough to allow play; give the whole of the skin inside a dressing with the arsenical paste (say of the consistency of cream), fill it with cotton wool, until it is once more of the natural size, and then it may be sewn up. To do this properly, take a needleful of linen thread, insert the needle at one side of the breast (always insert from the inside), leaving one end of the thread hanging down beyond the tail (the reason of this will be seen later), then insert the needle in the same way on the other side, and so on, across and across, until you reach the tail. Do not draw each stitch tight, but leave the skin open until you have taken the last stitch, and then each stitch may be drawn up tight by simply lifting it with the knitting-needle, just in the same way as you would lace up a boot or a football, with the aid of a button-hook. The end of the thread which was allowed to hang down is now tied to the other end, close to the skin, in a double knot, and it then becomes impossible for the skin to re-open unless the thread be cut. Lift the breast-feathers into their proper places with the finger and thumb. Brush the skin all over with cotton wool to remove any plaster there may be upon it (which, by the way, will not stick to the feathers unless they are wet), and the operation is complete. Nothing remains but to put the skin in shape and allow it to dry. Many persons, after getting thus far, fail at the last moment to give the skin a natural shape and appearance. This can only be acquired by practice and acquaintance with the structure of the particular bird which is being operated upon. Having adjusted the wings in their proper place, a band of paper and a pin will keep them in position until the skin is dry. With the aid of the knitting-needle the plumage is very easily put in order, and nothing more is requisite, except to take care that no one shall touch it until it is dry. If you are obliged to travel before your skins are dry, you run the risk of putting them all out of shape. In this case they should be unpacked every night and re-arranged.

It need not be supposed that because a bird has been skinned it is rendered unfit for eating. This is not the case. Some birds with thick oily skins are all the better without them. As a rule, a bird is not improved by being skinned, for it is rendered dry in consequence; but, at the same time, as the body is invariably removed before any arsenic is applied to the skin, and as the plaster-of-Paris—which is perfectly harmless—will always wash off, the bird is really as palatable as ever. There will probably be no difficulty in procuring a lemon in the village, and a small bottle of cayenne is easily carried in your portmanteau. A dish of roasted plovers, greenshanks, or knots, with these adjuncts, is by no means to be despised. Indeed, we have found from experience that hunger is the best sauce, and he who has thoroughly devoted himself all day to the sport we have described will assuredly not be fastidious when the dinner hour arrives.

As a receipt for health and strength nothing can equal a good day's shore shooting. It exercises the body, improves the mind, and thus, while providing recreation, provides also an increase to knowledge. Nor does the pleasure end with the excursion. He

who has occupied his evenings in preserving some of
the many beautiful birds he has met with, will carry
home with him mementoes which can never fail to
delight him as often as he looks at them, recalling
to his mind, as they will do, many a good day's
sport.

Woodfall and Kinder, Printers, Milford Lane, Strand, London, W.C.

www.ingramcontent.com/pod-product-compliance
Lightning Source LLC
Chambersburg PA
CBHW020032030726
47499CB00007B/2382